THE WORST WITCH STRIKES AGAIN

DATE DUE

By the same author

THE WORST WITCH
A BAD SPELL FOR THE WORST WITCH

THE WORST WITCH STRIKES AGAIN

Written and illustrated by Jill Murphy

VIKING KESTREL

VIKING KESTREL

Published by the Penguin Group
27 Wrights Lane, London w8 5TZ, England
Viking Penguin Inc., 40 West 23rd Street, New York, New York 10010, USA
Penguin Books Australia Ltd, Ringwood, Victoria, Australia
Penguin Books Canada Ltd, 2801 John Street, Markham, Ontario, Canada L3R 1B4
Penguin Books (NZ) Ltd, 182–190 Wairau Road, Auckland 10, New Zealand

Penguin Books Ltd, Registered Offices: Harmondsworth, Middlesex, England

First published by Allison & Busby 1980
Published in Puffin Books 1981
Published by Viking Kestrel 1988
3 5 7 9 10 8 6 4 2

Made and printed in Great Britain by
Richard Clay Ltd, Bungay, Suffolk
Filmset in Monophoto Baskerville

British Library Cataloguing in Publication Data available

ISBN 0-670-82189-6

For
Luc,
and
Isabelle

SUMMER had arrived at Miss Cackle's Academy for Witches. Not that it made much difference to the grim-looking school which was perched on a mountain amid swirling mist and pine trees.

On the first morning of term the members of Form One sat in class looking a dismal sight in their new summer uniform which was even more dreary than the winter one. It consisted of a black-and-

grey-checked short-sleeved dress, bright-
ened a little by the sash around the waist,
and grey ankle socks with black lace-up
shoes. Everyone's knees were startlingly
white after spending the winter swathed
in itchy black wool stockings.

Despite this picture of gloom, the room
buzzed with laughing voices and the
pupils all sounded very excited to be back
– except for Mildred. Worried would be a
better word to describe how Mildred felt
as she sat on her desk listening to Maud's
tales of what had happened during the
holidays.

In fact, she wasn't really listening to
Maud at all because she was busy imagining all the dreadful things that were just
bound to happen during the coming term.
Why, it hadn't even *started* yet. There were
weeks and weeks to get through! After the
appalling report she'd had at the end of
last term, she had promised everyone at
home that she *really would try* this term.

Even though Miss Cackle had kindly mentioned the day when she had saved the school from disaster, it hardly made up for all the days when everything she touched fell to bits or broke or, worse, when she couldn't resist doing something wicked to liven things up a bit. It was the worst report she'd ever taken home.

'Mildred!' Maud broke into her thoughts. 'You haven't been listening to a word, have you?'

'Yes, I have,' said Mildred.

'Well, what did I say then?' asked Maud.

'Er – you got a pet bat for your birthday?' replied Mildred, hopefully.

'I told you you weren't listening!' cried Maud triumphantly. 'That was about ten minutes ago.'

The door crashed open and Miss Hard-broom, their terrifying form-mistress, swept in like an icy blast, bringing with her a girl whom no one had ever seen

before. As usual, everyone nearly jumped out of their skins, and there was a mad scramble as desk-lids slammed and people crashed into each other in their hurry to be standing by their desks in an orderly manner.

10

'Good morning, girls,' said Miss Hardbroom crisply.

'Good morning, Miss Hardbroom,' replied the girls.

'I hope you're all glad to be back with us,' said Miss Hardbroom, narrowing her eyes and glaring at the unfortunate pupils in the front row. 'All nice and rested and looking forward to some hard work?'

'Yes, Miss Hardbroom,' chorused the girls in their most sincere voices.

'Good!' said Miss Hardbroom, clapping her hands together in a business-like way. 'Now then. This is Enid Nightshade.' She extended a bony hand towards the newcomer, who stood with hunched shoulders, looking fixedly at the floor.

Enid was a tall girl, even taller than Mildred, but much more ungainly, with big hands and feet. There seemed to be an awful lot of her, though she wasn't exactly fat. Her hair was the colour of milky tea and was restrained into a long, thick plait,

12

but you could tell that it would be very wild and wavy once it was unleashed from the black hair ribbon.

'Enid is newly with us this term,' said Miss Hardbroom. 'Mildred, Enid is to be entrusted to your care. I must point out that this is not my idea, but some strange notion of Miss Cackle's that if you are awarded such a responsibility it may actually turn you into a responsible member of the community. Personally, I feel it a great loss to send young Enid off down the path of ill-fame with you, when we could all breathe easily if someone like Ethel were to show her the ropes.'

Ethel, the form sneak and goody-goody, smiled demurely at this point and everyone felt like hitting her.

'However,' continued Miss Hardbroom, 'perhaps I shall be proved wrong. I certainly hope so. Please make sure that Enid knows where everything is, Mildred, and keep her company for the next few days.

Thank you. Now, Enid, take the desk next to Mildred and let us begin the lesson. The first school assembly will be tomorrow morning in the Great Hall.'

'Crumbs,' thought Mildred, sneaking a look at Enid, who had crammed her huge frame into the neighbouring desk. 'We won't get much fun out of *her*.'

But Mildred couldn't have been more wrong.

EARLY next morning before the rising-
bell had rung, Maud crept along
the stone corridor to Mildred's room
and knocked on the door.

There was no reply, but this was hardly
surprising as Mildred was renowned for
her ability to sleep through any amount
of noise; in fact Maud often had to go and

shriek in her friend's ear to waken her when the rising-bell failed to do so.

Maud tiptoed into the room, closing the heavy door quietly behind her. Mildred's three bats skimmed over her head returning from their night out and settled upside-down on the picture rail.

A soft 'Miaaow' at her feet reminded Maud of Mildred's little tabby cat which was threading itself round her ankles. She bent down and picked up the little creature, which immediately draped itself around her neck like a fur stole and began to purr. Maud was quite glad of the warmth as she felt a bit chilly in her summer nightdress of grey cotton.

'Mildred,' she whispered to the bundle of bedclothes. 'Wake up, Mildred. It's Maud.'

'Whassat?' mumbled Mildred's voice from deep under the covers, followed by a series of rhythmic snores.

'*Mildred*!' whispered Maud, giving the

lump under the covers a vigorous shake.
'Wake up!'

The top of Mildred's head appeared on
the pillow.

'Oh, hello, Maud!' she said. 'Is it time to
get up yet? Did I miss the bell?'

'No,' said Maud curling up on the end
of the bed. 'It's still early. The bats have
only just come in. I came to have a chat
before the others get up.'

Mildred hauled herself into a sitting position.

'Wrap yourself up, you must be freezing,' she said, offering Maud her black cloak. Maud took the cloak from the bedpost and put it around her shoulders.

'Thanks,' she said. 'What shall we do at break?'

'Well,' said Mildred, 'I've got to show Enid round the school. You know, the potion lab and gym, that sort of thing.'

'Can't you hand her over to someone else?' asked Maud, sounding a little touchy. 'She looks very dull, and anyway you and *I* always go about together.'

'It's a bit difficult to get rid of her,' said Mildred. 'Miss Hardbroom asked me and she'd go berserk if I tried to get out of it. Anyway the poor girl is new, I feel a bit sorry for her.'

'Oh, all right,' agreed Maud reluctantly. 'I'll come and call for you later and we can at least go to Assembly together.'

'Er – well, I'll have to take Enid to Assembly,' said Mildred awkwardly. 'But you can come too, though.'

'Oh, *thanks*!' stormed Maud. 'I'd rather go on my own.' She flung off the cloak and uncurled the cat. 'Perhaps you could fit me in later in the week!'

'Oh, Maud!' said Mildred. 'Don't be so silly, I didn't mean –'

But Maud had already swept out of the door, letting it bang behind her.

TEN minutes later, the rising-bell clanged and echoed through the gloomy corridors. Mildred, who was just on the verge of going back to sleep, steeled herself to get out of bed and grope around for her clothes which were festooned all over the room as usual. The summer dress was much easier to cope with than the winter uniform. Somehow, in winter she always got in a dreadful muddle with her tie.

She was just about to go and bang on Maud's door and surprise her by being ready when she remembered about Enid and set off to the next corridor to call for her.

'Enid! Are you up yet?' she called softly through the door.

'Hang on a sec!' called Enid's voice. 'I'm just feeding the monkey.'

'Monkey?' thought Mildred. 'I must have misheard.'

But she hadn't. When she pushed open the door, there sat Enid on her narrow bedstead. Perched on her shoulder was a slender grey monkey eating a banana.

'It's to go on the back of my broom,' explained Enid, as Mildred hastened inside and closed the door, in case by some mischance Miss Hardbroom should materialize outside.

'But it's a *monkey*, Enid!' exclaimed Mildred. 'You won't be allowed. It says in the rules that we can only have cats. We can't even have owls.'

'Oh, it'll be all right,' said Enid airily. 'No one'll notice when it's all hunched up on the end of my broom.'

I wouldn't be too sure,' said Mildred

darkly. 'You don't know Miss Hardbroom yet.'

'Anyway,' continued Enid as if she hadn't heard Mildred's dire warning, 'it's much more fun than a silly old cat. It can hang upside-down by its tail and do all sorts of things.'

'Well,' said Mildred doubtfully, 'I do hope it'll be all right. Come on, we'd better go down to Assembly or we'll be late, and that would never do when I'm supposed to be looking after you!'

As the girls filed into the Great Hall, Mildred caught Maud by the arm and whispered, 'Hey, Maud! You'll never guess what Enid has got in her room.'

But Maud didn't answer and brushed past with her nose in the air.

Miss Hardbroom stood beside the head-mistress, Miss Cackle, on the platform at the end of the Great Hall. Unlike Miss Hardbroom who was scowling, Miss Cackle beamed down at her flock which

stood in neat black-and-grey-checked rows
in front of her. Mildred could not suppress
a snigger at the strange-looking pair they
made. Miss Cackle short and wearing a
tight dress of grey satin which made her
look very bulgy, and Miss Hardbroom
tall and extremely thin, wearing a gown

with black vertical stripes which made her look even taller.

Miss Hardbroom's piercing gaze swept past like a searchlight, causing Mildred's smile to vanish instantly like the sun behind a cloud.

'Welcome back, girls,' said Miss Cackle. 'You have a term of hard work ahead of you. As well as the usual exams there will be the school Sports Day which I know you all look forward to.'

At this point Miss Hardbroom closed her eyes and a look of pain flashed across her face. Mildred also felt a twinge of dread as she remembered the disastrous broomstick display at Hallowe'en the year before.

Now Miss Cackle looked a little shy. 'And there will be my birthday celebration

when I look forward to the little songs and chants which you always prepare for me.'

A gentle groan ran round the room. Miss Cackle's birthday celebration was the most boring event of the year.

AFTER Assembly the girls marched to the music-room for their chanting lesson with Miss Bat the chanting mistress. She was tiny, thin and very old with frizzy grey hair which she wore in a plait twisted around the back of her head. Because of her habit of pressing her jaw into her chest, she had three chins and this looked very odd on top of her thin little figure. She wore circular steel glasses attached to a chain round her neck (not the dainty gold kind but more like a bicycle chain) and she always had a conductor's baton tucked behind her ear.

She sat at the piano in a black dress with grey flowers and played a rousing march as the girls entered.

'Chanting's ever so dull,' whispered Mildred to Enid as they marched into the music-room.

'Don't you believe it,' Enid whispered back with a surprisingly wicked glint in her eye.

They all took their places, and Mildred managed to position herself with Maud on one side and Enid on the other, though Maud still looked very crochety and wouldn't return Mildred's smile.

Miss Bat struck up the opening chord to a chant that they all knew very well, and the girls began.

To Mildred's surprise, Enid was singing completely out of tune – not loud enough for Miss Bat to hear, but loud enough so that Mildred couldn't concentrate on the right note herself. Verse after verse droned on with Enid just missing the correct note and the pupils around her struggling to keep in tune.

Mildred sneaked a look at Enid, who was smiling sweetly and obviously doing it on purpose, then glanced at Maud who was trying desperately to keep a straight

face. A sudden mad burst of uncontrollable laughter welled up in Mildred. She clenched her teeth and racked her brains to think of something sad, but the sound of Enid's voice droning flatly on beside her was too much and a loud snorting noise erupted from Mildred's nose like a motor-bike starting up.

Mildred put her hands across her mouth and even tried stuffing her handkerchief into it, but it was no use, a real fit of the giggles was upon her and she just doubled up with helpless laughter and giggled till her face ached.

'Mildred Hubble!' The inevitable words rang out across the room in a tone which implied that Miss Bat would stand no more nonsense. Everyone had stopped chanting, and Mildred's peals of laughter echoed embarrassingly round the silent walls.

'Come out here at once!' ordered Miss Bat.

Mildred clumped through the rows of

pupils and stood next to the piano. She took
a deep breath and managed to look serious,
though her face was flaming and the sound
of Enid's voice still resounded in her head.

When Miss Bat was angry there were

two things she always did. First, her head would begin nodding (which it was doing now) and, secondly, she would take the baton from behind her ear and begin conducting an invisible orchestra (which she was also doing now). Mildred could tell that she was furious.

'What, may I ask, is so hilarious that you are prepared to disrupt the entire chanting lesson for the sake of it?' inquired Miss Bat coldly. 'No one else seems to be laughing. Perhaps you would let us all in on the joke!'

Mildred stole a glance at Maud and Enid. Maud was staring intently at her feet, and Enid was gazing at the ceiling, the picture of innocence.

'It was –' began Mildred, but a splutter of laughter came out and she dissolved into a giggling wreck again.

At last the wave subsided and she was left breathless, but able to speak.

'*Now*, Mildred,' quavered Miss Bat, in a

voice like a taut violin string, 'I'm waiting for a reasonable explanation.'

'Enid was singing out of tune,' said Mildred.

'Well!' said Miss Bat. 'I hardly think that is a reason for such a display of appalling manners. Come here, Enid my dear.'

Enid came and stood next to Mildred by the piano.

'Now, my dear,' said Miss Bat kindly, 'you must not feel shy because you can't sing very well. I hope you are not too upset just because Mildred decided to make a spectacle of herself on your account. Now, let me hear you sing one or two bars of "Eye of Toad" and we shall see if we can help you along a little.'

Enid obliged in the same wavering, off-key voice as before,

'Eye of toad,
Ear of bat,

Leg of frog,
Tail of cat.
Drop them in,
Stir it up,
Pour it in a silver cup.'

This was the last straw for Mildred, who abandoned all efforts at keeping control and gave herself up to complete hysteria.

As you may imagine, it was also the last straw for Miss Bat, and Mildred found herself on her way to the headmistress's office for the first time that term.

MISS CACKLE was not pleased when Mildred entered her study.

'Good morning, Mildred,' she said wearily, motioning the hapless pupil to sit down. 'I suppose it is too much to hope for that you are sent here with a message, or for some innocent reason?'

'Yes, Miss Cackle,' murmured Mildred. 'Miss Bat sent me to you because I was laughing in the chanting lesson. One of my friends was singing out of tune and I couldn't stop laughing.'

Miss Cackle looked at Mildred over the top of her spectacles and Mildred wondered why Enid's singing didn't sound in the least bit funny now, in front of the headmistress.

'I wonder,' said Miss Cackle, 'if there is any hope at all for you in this Academy. You take one pace forward then four paces backward; it's the same old story, Mildred, isn't it? And the term's only just begun. I see that Miss Hardbroom was right when she disagreed with my plan to put you in charge of the new girl. I have put you in a position of responsibility, Mildred, and you must live up to it, not let me down.'

'Yes, Miss Cackle,' agreed Mildred fervently.

'It would be a sad thing indeed,' continued Miss Cackle, 'if you were to lead this innocent new pupil up the garden path with you, would it not? Now, child, for the last time, pull yourself together and let me hear no more about you for the rest of the term.'

Mildred assured Miss Cackle of her good intentions and meekly left the room.

As there was still a good hour of chanting left and Miss Bat had told her not to come back, Mildred decided to sneak up to Enid's room and take a look at the monkey.

Mildred could hear her fellow-pupils chanting in the music-room as she crept up the spiral staircase to Enid's room. It gave her a delicious sense of freedom to have a whole hour stretched before her while everyone else in the school was imprisoned in a stuffy classroom.

For once the sun had filtered through the shroud of mist, and shafts of sunlight fell dramatically through the slit-windows on to the cool stone steps.

'Well, I certainly made a mistake about Enid,' thought Mildred. 'She's worse than I am.'

She giggled again at the thought of the

tuneless chanting and opened the door of Enid's room.

As she did so the monkey, which had been sitting on the bedpost, made a dive for the door straight over Mildred's head and off down the corridor screeching with delight. Mildred saw its long tail whip round the corner as it plunged down the spiral staircase.

'Oh, no!' thought Mildred, setting off after the creature as fast as she could.

She arrived breathless at the bottom of the staircase, only to find that the monkey was nowhere to be seen.

'Oh, dear,' she muttered aloud. 'What *am* I going to do?'

'What *should* you be doing, Mildred?' asked a chilling voice behind her.

'Oh! Er – nothing, Miss Hardbroom,' replied Mildred, for it was her form-mistress who had appeared from nowhere.

'Nothing,' echoed Miss Hardbroom frostily. 'At this time of day? Why, I ask myself, should Mildred Hubble be hurtling around the corridors when everyone else is usefully employed in a lesson somewhere? And why, I ask myself, should Mildred Hubble's socks be trailing round her ankles?'

Mildred bent down and hastily pulled them up.

'I was sent out of chanting, Miss Hardbroom,' she explained. 'Miss Bat told me not to come back so I've got nothing to do for the next hour.'

'*Nothing to do*?' exploded Miss Hardbroom, her eyes flashing so wildly that Mildred backed away. 'Well, I would suggest that you take yourself to the library and brush up on your spells and potions for a start, and then perhaps if there is any time left – which I doubt – you can come and find me in my room and I will give you a test on what you have learned.'

'Yes, Miss Hardbroom,' said Mildred.

Desperately trying to work out where the monkey could have got to, Mildred took the corridor which led towards the library. She looked back over her shoulder and saw that Miss Hardbroom had vanished, which was very confusing as you were never sure if she was watching invisible, or if she had walked away.

Mildred walked on for a few more corridors, then waited and listened. All she could hear was the faint chanting of Form One in the distance, so she set off in search of the lost monkey again.

Something moving caught her eye through one of the windows. It was the monkey, halfway up one of the towers,

swinging about by its tail. It had managed
to get hold of a hat from somewhere and
was wearing it rammed down over its ears.
If Mildred hadn't been quite so horrified
she would have seen how funny the animal
looked.

'Oh, come down, Monkey, please!' she
called as softly as possible. 'I've got a nice
banana for you.'

But the monkey only let out a shriek and
climbed a bit higher. Mildred ran as fast as
she could and fetched her broomstick. As

far as she could see, the only way to get the monkey down was to fly across and catch it.

Nervously she stepped on to the window-ledge and lowered herself on to the broomstick. She gave the command for it to fly, but unfortunately, as she gave it a tap (which was the signal for it to start), she slipped and the broom zoomed off with Mildred hanging on by her arms.

'Stop!' yelled Mildred, at which the

broom stopped and hovered in mid-air. Mildred tried to haul herself on to it, but that was impossible with nothing to push her feet against. Her arms were practically out of their sockets, but she was so near the monkey that she decided to give it a try and commanded the stick to fly on. As luck would have it, the monkey was

fascinated by the sight of the broom and jumped on to it, where it proceeded to run up and down and swing by its tail.

'Down!' Mildred commanded the broom and the extraordinary little group whooshed downwards.

As they came in to land, Mildred was shocked to see that the yard was full of people. Form Three had been having a broomstick lesson with Miss Drill the gymmistress, and had witnessed the whole episode on the tower. Even worse, Miss Hardbroom was standing next to Miss Drill with her arms folded and both eyebrows raised. Mildred felt quite ridiculous as she floated to the ground in such an ungainly position with the monkey swinging beside her.

'Well?' asked Miss Hardbroom, as Mildred took the monkey from the broom and stood holding it tightly in case it should escape.

'I – er – I found it!' exclaimed Mildred.

45

'On the tower,' sneered Miss Hardbroom, 'wearing a hat.'

'Yes,' said Mildred, almost dying of embarrassment. 'It was up there so I ... thought I ought to bring it down.'

'And where did it come from?' demanded Miss Hardbroom, narrowing her eyes. 'You haven't been arguing with Ethel again, have you?' (She was thinking of the time last term when Mildred had changed Ethel into a pig during an argument.)

'No, Miss Hardbroom!' said Mildred.

'Well, then, Mildred, where did you get the monkey from?'

This was a very tricky situation. Mildred could not possibly sneak on Enid but Miss Hardbroom's terrifying stare made Mildred feel that she probably knew anyway. Perhaps it was just as well that a member of Form Three stepped forward.

'She got it from the new girl's room'

announced the girl. 'I saw her coming out of there earlier on.'

'Enid's room?' queried Miss Hardbroom. 'But Enid has a regulation black cat. There is no other animal in her room.'

She sent the girl to fetch Enid from the chanting lesson and Enid soon arrived looking bewildered. She did not flinch when she saw Mildred with the monkey.

'Is this your monkey, Enid?' asked Miss Hardbroom.

'I only have a cat, Miss Hardbroom,' replied Enid.

Mildred's eyes widened in disbelief.

'Are you *quite* sure it isn't Ethel?' asked Miss Hardbroom severely.

'Yes, Miss Hardbroom,' said Mildred.

Miss Hardbroom, however, did not believe her and she muttered the spell which would change the animal back to its original form. To Mildred's surprise the monkey vanished and in its place stood a little black cat.

'That's my cat!' cried Enid, as the cat jumped into her arms.

'Mildred!' said Miss Hardbroom, 'you've been told about this before. First Ethel, now Enid's cat. For goodness' sake, when is this nonsense going to stop?'

Mildred was astonished.

'But Miss – I –' she gasped.

'Silence,' said Miss Hardbroom. 'Two days you have been back at school and already twice in disgrace. At least this encounter has allowed Enid to see what a bad example you are. I hope you will take care not to follow in Mildred's footsteps, Enid. Now run along, both of you, and *take care*, Mildred. Just think before you embark on such an escapade again.'

The minute the two girls were round the corner Mildred asked Enid what on earth was going on.

'Simple,' said Enid, 'it really *is* my cat. I changed it into a monkey before breakfast this morning, for fun. I was going to

change it back tomorrow when we go for
Sports Day practice. I didn't know you
were going to go and let it out, did I?'

SPORTS DAY loomed ahead like a black cloud for Mildred, as did anything where competition was called for. She hated the idea of trying to beat other people, mainly because she never won and it was all so humiliating, but also because it just wasn't her way of doing things.

As well as this, Maud was being very trying. Just because Mildred had been put in charge of Enid, which meant that she *had* to take Enid around with her, Maud had gone off in a jealous huff and had even gone as far as teaming up with Ethel.

Mildred could hardly believe it when she saw the two of them together. She knew Maud was just doing it because of Enid, so she pretended not to take any notice, but in fact it nearly killed her to see her best friend arm-in-arm with her old enemy.

There were various events on the Sports Day agenda: pole-vaulting, sack-racing, cat-balancing, relay broomstick-racing, and a prize for the best trained cat.

Everyone practised very hard in the

weeks leading up to the Sports Day. Mildred had long sessions with her little tabby cat trying to teach it to sit up straight instead of hanging on with its eyes shut, but little progress was made. Mildred and Enid ran races against each other and always tied but this was no indication of merit as they were equally bad.

The weeks soon slid by and Sports Day dawned grey and misty. For once Mildred was wide awake when the rising-bell sounded, as she had been tossing and turning for most of the night with dreadful nightmares. One was about finding a monster on the back of her broom in the middle of the relay-race and it turned into Miss Cackle who said, 'Mildred! You've done it again!'

As the first peals of the bell rang out, Mildred dragged herself out of bed and rummaged around for her sports kit. She found it crumpled up at the bottom of her sock drawer and tried to smooth it out so it would look a bit more presentable.

Some mornings were worse than others, she reflected, as she pulled on the dingy grey aertex shirt and black divided skirt which hung limply to her knees. The grey socks and black plimsolls completed the picture of gloom as she plaited her hair tightly.

There was a knock at the door and for a happy moment she thought it must be Maud, but Enid put her head round the door and Mildred remembered Maud had gone off with Ethel.

'Don't laugh,' said Enid as she brought the rest of herself into the room.

Mildred obliged with a snort of mirth at the sight of Enid's sports kit.

'I said *don't* laugh,' said Enid smiling. 'I know they're funny, but I haven't got a proper pair.'

She was wearing a vast pair of black knickers which were pulled up under her arms.

'Haven't you got a smaller pair?' asked Mildred.

'No,' replied Enid. 'My mother buys everything with growing room because I'm so big. You should see my vests! Some of them trail on the floor when they aren't tucked in.'

'I shan't be able to keep a straight face with you in those,' said Mildred. 'Still, it might put the others off. How's your cat?'

'I'm not bringing it,' said Enid. 'It's been a bit off-colour since the monkey

incident. I don't think it could cope with broomstick riding.'

'I'm bringing Tabby,' said Mildred, taking the cat from its position curled up on the pillow. 'I've been training it every day, but I don't know if it's done any good.'

ENID and Mildred sat in the cloakroom waiting to be called for the first event, which was the pole-vault. To their great consternation they discovered that they had been entered for everything, mainly because they were both so tall, and this gave rise to the completely false idea that they must be good at sports.

'We're *bound* to come last,' said Enid despairingly.

'We don't have to,' said Mildred, stroking the tabby cat's head which was sticking

58

out of the top of her shoe-bag. 'We're taller than everyone else, we *ought* to be better than them.'

'*Exactly*,' said Enid miserably. 'But we aren't. What we need is a touch of magic.'

'Oh, Enid,' said Mildred anxiously. 'I can't even do *that* properly. You weren't here when I made the wrong potion in the potion-lab and Maud and I disappeared. It was dreadful.'

'Leave it to me,' said Enid with disarming confidence.

Mildred watched as her friend took the two poles to the window and waved her arms around them muttering words under her breath.

'What are you doing?' asked Mildred.

'Shhh,' said Enid. 'You'll mess up the spell.'

A minute later, Enid handed Mildred's pole back to her ...

'Come on,' she said. 'We'll beat the lot of them now.'

Mildred felt distinctly uneasy as they joined the contestants for the pole-vault. She looked up at the bar which seemed to be at least a mile high.

'I'll never get over that,' she whispered to Enid.

'Mildred Hubble!' announced Miss Drill.

'Oh, no!' gasped Mildred. 'I'm first.'

'Just jump,' said Enid with a wink. 'You'll be all right.'

So Mildred jumped. She charged along the run-up strip, banged the pole on to the groud and, as she did so, an extraordinary thing happened. The ground suddenly seemed to be made of a strong, springy material, and both Mildred and the pole went soaring up into the air.

From somewhere far below she heard Enid shout, 'Let go of the pole!'

Glancing down, Mildred saw to her horror that everything was way below her, including the pole-vault bar and the school

walls. She was so shocked that she hung
on even more tightly and saw that a turret
was looming up in front of her with
gathering speed. Like a guided missile,

Mildred and the pole shot straight through
one of the windows (fortunately the castle-
like school did not have glass in any of
them) and crash-landed in the middle of a
table all set out ready for somebody's tea.

Lying dazed on the floor amid shattered
teacups and pools of milk, Mildred saw to
her dismay that she had hurled herself into
Miss Hardbroom's private study. The pole

was neatly broken in two with one half
embedded in a portrait of Miss Hardbroom, and the other half in the cat basket,
having just missed Miss Hardbroom's cat,
now snarling and spitting on top of a
cupboard.

It wasn't very long before the door

opened and Miss Hardbroom, Miss Cackle and Miss Drill all came bursting in through the door. The terrified cat leapt on to its owner's shoulders with a yowl.

64

'Nice of you to drop in, Mildred,' sneered Miss Hardbroom. 'However, it was hardly necessary to use such an unorthodox method of getting here. Everyone else seems to find the stairs perfectly adequate.'

'I'm sure I do not have to remind you, Mildred,' said Miss Drill, 'that it is against the rules to use magic in any sporting event.'

'I just cannot understand it,' sighed Miss Cackle, removing a squashed jam tart from Mildred's hair and absentmindedly feeding it to Miss Hardbroom's cat.

'I can hardly believe that one of my girls would cheat, and that poor new girl witnessing such an example. Shocking, shocking.'

Mildred silently ground her teeth when she thought of the number of times 'the poor new girl' had got her into trouble since term began.

'This *must* be positively the last time that

anything of this sort happens,' said Miss Cackle sternly. 'You are disqualified from the rest of the events, and if I see you in trouble even once more this term then I shall have to disqualify you from the school itself.'

Mildred gasped.

'Yes, Mildred,' Miss Cackle continued, 'I shall be forced to expel you if this reckless behaviour continues. Now go to

your room for the rest of the day and ponder upon all I have told you.'

Mildred was only too glad to escape to her room. She curled up on her bed with the little cat and listened to the rest of the school laughing and cheering outside as Sports Day continued.

'It's impossible, Tabby,' she said. 'I shall never get right through to the end of term without *anything* happening.'

There was a tap at the door and in came Enid.

'What happened?' she asked. 'Where did you land?'

'Oh, it was awful!' said Mildred. 'I ended up in Miss Hardbroom's study. Miss Cackle said she'll expel me if I do anything else this term. What about you? Did you go too high as well?'

'Oh, no,' said Enid. 'I realized that I must have over-magicked the poles, so I pretended to faint and got sent off to the rest-room. I'll have to nip back in a minute. Did you get hurt?'

'Not much,' said Mildred ruefully. 'Just twisted my ankle a bit. I'm all right.'

'Well, cheer up,' said Enid brightly, opening the door. 'At least nothing else can go wrong today. I'll see you later.'

Mildred managed a weak smile as Enid disappeared into the corridor.

'Oh, Tabby,' she said miserably to the little cat. 'We've got one more chance, that's all.'

ILDRED had not felt so anxious about being expelled since the day when she had ruined the broomstick formation team at Hallowe'en. She remembered all the promises to her family about being good, and thought how dreadful it would be if she arrived home with her cat and suitcases to break the dreadful news to them. She looked at her calendar and decided to struggle through each day as it came, making every effort to reach the end of term without any more incidents.

Enid tried to tempt her to every imaginable escapade during the weeks that followed, but with admirable strength of mind Mildred resisted. Ethel was being particularly provoking because Maud was still her friend, but Mildred withstood all teasing and managed to battle through to the last week of term without any more trouble at all.

Miss Cackle's birthday celebration was to be held as usual on the last day of term and each class had chosen a little chant or poem to be performed on the day. Maud had been chosen to represent Form One and Mildred was relieved not to be involved apart from having to sit and listen.

'This is going to be awful,' announced Enid as they sat in class waiting to be called to the Great Hall. 'Why don't we skip it? I don't know if I can stand a whole morning of recitation.'

'No,' replied Mildred flatly.

'Oh, go on, Mil,' said Enid persuasively. 'You aren't any fun any more. No one is going to see if we sneak off. The whole school's there. No one will notice if *we* aren't.'

'They will, and I'm not,' said Mildred. 'I've only got another three or four hours to get through, then I can go home for the holidays without being expelled. I just can't risk it.'

'Oh, all right,' agreed Enid sounding very disgruntled.

Miss Hardbroom appeared in the doorway and signalled the class to march down to the Great Hall. As they filed down the corridor Enid suddenly grabbed Mildred's arm.

'Quick!' she hissed. 'In here!'

They were passing a store cupboard at the time, and before Mildred knew what had happened Enid had dived inside, pulling Mildred with her.

'What on earth are you doing?' whispered Mildred as Enid hastily closed the door.

'Shhh,' said Enid. 'All we have to do is to stay in here till they're all in the Assembly Hall, then we can go off and spend the morning as we like.'

'But – oh, Enid!' said Mildred hopelessly. 'We're bound to get caught.'

Meanwhile outside, Ethel's eagle eye had seen Mildred and Enid vanishing into the cupboard; so had Maud, who secretly wished she had been with them. Life had been such fun with Mildred as her best friend, and a whole term in Ethel's

company had been very unpleasant indeed, especially as Ethel *would* keep going on about how dreadful Mildred was.

As Maud and Ethel passed by the cupboard, Ethel turned the key and locked the door.

'Ethel!' said Maud as they marched on into the Assembly Hall. 'That was mean. You'll get them into trouble. Miss Cackle said she'd expel Mildred if she did anything else.'

'Exactly,' said Ethel triumphantly.

'I think you're a beast,' said Maud. 'I'm going to creep back and let them out.'

But at that moment Miss Hardbroom swept along the corridor and escorted Maud's section of the line into the hall, so there was no way in which she could get back to unlock the cupboard door.

Inside the cupboard, the two young witches heard the key turn.

'I knew it,' said Mildred. 'We can't get out now and it's the last day of term. We'll

have to bang on the door when they all
come out of the hall or we'll be in here for
the whole of the holiday. They'll open the
door at the beginning of next term and
all they'll find will be a little heap of bones.'

Mildred burst into tears at this distress-
ing thought.

'Oh, Mil, I am sorry,' said Enid. 'I'll
tell them it's my fault. Don't cry. You
won't be expelled, I promise.'

WHEN their eyes had become accustomed to the dim light in the cupboard, Mildred and Enid looked around and saw that they were in a very large, high-ceilinged room which was obviously used for storing old furniture. The light was filtering in from an arched window high up in one corner.

'We're saved!' shrieked Enid, snapping her fingers. 'There's a window. All we have to do is get up there.'

'Oh, that's easy,' said Mildred sarcastically. 'It's only about ten feet up the wall. Why don't we fly?'

'Perhaps we could pile some of these things and climb up,' said Enid desperately, rummaging through the old desks, broken benches and cardboard boxes full of rubbish. 'Look, Mildred!' she exclaimed. 'It's a broomstick!'

She hauled from a wooden chest an ancient broomstick, almost snapped in two but for a few splinters of wood still holding it together. Enid took off her sash and bound it as tightly as possible.

'There!' she said. 'Now we *can* fly up. The window looks big enough for us both to squeeze out of. Come on.'

They commanded the broomstick to hover, which it did, and the two worst witches in the school balanced themselves on it. Enid sat in front and Mildred hung on round her waist. They made the broom rise like a helicopter which is done by saying, 'Up, up, up!' over and over again until you get as high as you want to go. It is a very jerky process and the two witches found it very hard to stay on, but at last they reached the window-sill.

'What can you see on the other side?'

asked Enid, concentrating on keeping the broom steady.

Mildred peered through and saw a long indoor wall and part of a ceiling stretching away before her.

'That's odd,' she said to Enid, 'it isn't an outside window. It seems to lead into a huge stone room.'

'Well, we'd better go through before this broom gives up on us,' said Enid sneezing from the dust and cobwebs draped all over them. 'Duck your head as we go through.'

'I wonder where we'll come out?' mused Mildred as they flew awkwardly through the window.

SILENCE had been called in the Great
Hall. Maud, who was the first
performer, stood on the stage with
Miss Cackle and all the mistresses
behind her and the rest of the school facing
her in the lower part of the hall. She was
so worried about Mildred being locked in
the cupboard that she could not remember
the beginning of the poem though she had
been rehearsing it for weeks. As she stood

there wildly searching her memory, there was a loud sneeze and a strange scuffling sound at the back of the hall, and suddenly from a high window in the far corner Mildred and Enid came sailing out, covered in dust and holding on for dear life. The pupils all turned to look, and the teachers froze.

It took a split second for Maud to realize that she was not imagining things and that the window must face into the cupboard. Quick as a flash she cleared her throat.

'Miss Cackle and staff!' she announced importantly, her voice trembling. 'I am proud to announce a surprise item from Mildred Hubble and Enid Nightshade. A double broomstick display on a solo broomstick!'

She waved an arm in the direction of Mildred and Enid who looked positively thunderstruck when they realized exactly what they had flown into.

'I don't believe it,' muttered Mildred,

as every pair of eyes in the school turned
on the unlucky pair.

'If we manage to get out of this one, we
deserve a medal,' said Enid.

'Let's at least have a try, and do as Maud
said,' whispered Mildred. 'Hold the

broomstick steady and fly about a bit, and I'll do some fancy-work if I can.'

Enid started to fly the broom slowly round the hall and Mildred clambered up on to the back of it. Clinging on to Enid's shoulders, she managed to do an extremely wobbly arabesque. In fact she had never even stood up on a broomstick before and was rather pleased with herself. She did one with the other leg, and then got very daring and raised one arm up at the same time. Enid, who was not good at steering at the best of times, was not looking where she was going and saw the chandelier approaching just above her head.

'Mildred!' she exclaimed, but it was too late. Mildred crashed straight into it and Enid flew on leaving her friend dangling from the vast chandelier by one arm. She turned the broom and came back to pick Mildred up.

'That was a narrow squeak,' gasped Mildred, settling on to the broom. 'For

goodness' sake watch where you're going!'

'What?' said Enid, turning her head.

'I said watch out!' yelled Mildred as a wall came looming up in front of them.

Enid swerved violently and Mildred fell off just catching the broom by her fingertips and swinging in the air. At that moment, the long-suffering broomstick began to creak ominously in the middle where the sash was loosening.

'Quick, Enid!' said Mildred in despair.
'Take it in to land before it falls to bits!'

Enid guided the broom on to the stage
next to Maud who, with great presence of
mind began applauding, joined heartily by
the rest of the school.

Miss Cackle and Miss Hardbroom
stepped forward. Miss Cackle had a
slightly puzzled expression on her face, but
Miss Hardbroom had one eyebrow raised
like a dagger.

'Mildred Hubble,' she began in her most terrifying tone of voice, but before she could launch into the attack Miss Cackle put an arm around both Mildred's and Enid's shoulders.

'Thank you, children,' she said, smiling

short-sightedly through her horn-rimmed spectacles. 'Not very well executed, and the state of your clothing leaves much to be desired, but it was a good *try*. This is what we like to see in the Academy. Team spirit, initiative, but above all, *effort*.'

'Thank you, Miss Cackle,' said Mildred and Enid, not daring to look up in case they caught Miss Hardbroom's eye.

Miss Cackle smiled mistily and motioned the girls back to their seats. Of course there weren't any seats for Mildred and Enid who hadn't been there in the first place, but luckily benches had been used, so Maud squashed up and Enid and Mildred crammed in next to her.

As they filed out of the hall into the yard to wait for the bell which signalled the end of term, Maud told them about Ethel turning the key and the following events, and suddenly they all saw the funny side of it.

'Thanks, Maud,' giggled Mildred.

'It's all right,' said Maud awkwardly. 'Can we be friends again, Mildred?'

'We already are,' said Mildred, feeling a bit embarrassed. 'You've just saved us from a fate worse than death. Did you see her face?'

'*Whose* face, Mildred?' asked Miss Hardbroom's voice.

The three girls jumped in alarm as Miss

Hardbroom materialized in the doorway.

'I – I was just saying,' said Mildred, 'that we didn't do our surprise item very well and you didn't look too pleased.'

'I wasn't,' snapped Miss Hardbroom. 'However, I do think that the prize for initiative should go to Maud here. You have her to thank for saving you from a fate worse than death, whatever that may have been!'

She stood aside and waved a hand towards the sunny yard and the girls dived gratefully outside.

'She can see through walls,' whispered Maud.

'Shhh!' said Enid, glancing round. 'She really can.'

The bell rang out across the school telling the pupils that it was time to go and collect their cases. Mildred let out a cry of delight and danced her two friends round in a circle.

'I've done it!' she announced. 'It's the last day of term and I'm not expelled!'